little love

Rose Sprinkle
Illustrations by Crystal Ord

There once was a girl
With a hole in her heart.
Little Love was her name.
Where was she to start?

It was not of her doing.
She was not to blame.
But the hole in her heart
Was there just the same.

She tried to fill it
The best that she could,
But nothing made her happy,
Not a single thing would.

And so she set out
On her journey to find
The thing they call happy,
Her own peace of mind.

At first she met Fame, and oh how he glimmered.
The cameras, the spotlight, his riches that shimmered.

Maybe this is my happy.
Maybe this could be me.
I'll never feel lonely
With all eyes on me.

If fame wasn't what I thought it to be,
Maybe Beauty can fill this hole inside of me.

Beauty allured
and mesmerized many,
but her vain ambitions
Were much too demanding.

My flaws must be covered,
Every inch of them too.
If I'm to be loved,
Only perfect will do.

So Little Love plucked and puckered

and flattened and smoothed.

She buffed and shined and waxed through and through.

Then one day, Little Love
Looked in the mirror.
"Is that a reflection of me?"
She said with a tear.

"If Fame and Beauty cannot set me free
Then what can this world really offer to me?"

Then out of the mirror
Stepped a girl all in white.
Her face radiant and peaceful.
She shined oh so bright.

But not from the sparkles
Of an emerald or ruby,
Not from riches or fame,
Or even from beauty.

This light was different.
It came from within.
Its glow never wavered,
It was constant, not dim.

Little Love was perplexed.
She seemed so familiar.
The same eyes and nose,
It was all too peculiar.

And then, Little Love,
She suddenly knew,
How her heart could be happy,
How her heart could be new.

"This is my happy!
This is my true!
This light's within me!
I'm no different than you!"

"I made a mistake,
I saw only with sight,
The things the world tells me
I can never do right."

"There's beauty in many.
Not one is the same.
It's inside that matters,
Not fortune, or fame!"

And so, Little Love,
With small steps at first,
Filled up her whole heart,
So full it could burst!

With passion and knowledge
and wisdom and truth,

With patience and kindness

and charity, too.

And so, Little Love,
She learned in time,
The love in herself is
Always what shines.

COLLECT THEM ALL

www.thelittlevirtues.com

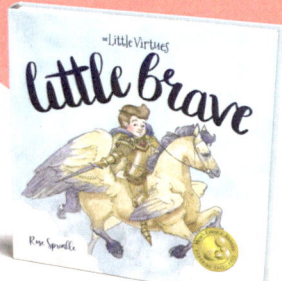

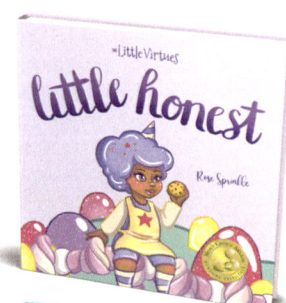
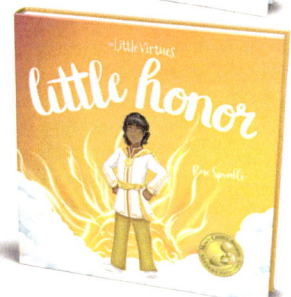
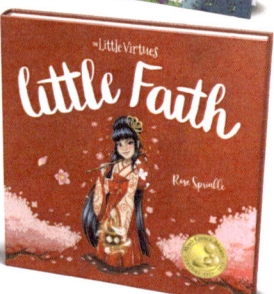

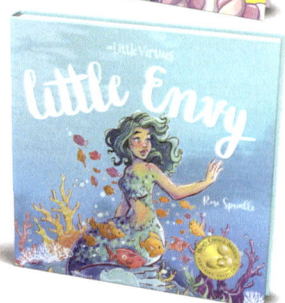

ABOUT THE AUTHOR
Rose Sprinkle started The Little Virtues to help kids develop emotional resilience and character. She's a mom who lives in the Pacific Northwest with her family and two frisky beagles. She loves creating stories and can't wait for you to be a part of The Little Virtues family.

 THELITTLEVIRTUESBOOKS

LITTLE LOVE. Copyright © 2024 The Little Virtues. All rights reserved.

Cataloguing-in-Publication data:

Sprinkle, Rose, Author | Ord, Crystal, Illustrator
Little Love / Rose Sprinkle.
ISBN 978-1-964896-01-4 (hardcover) | ISBN 978-1-964896-00-7 (paperback) | ISBN 978-1-964896-02-1 (ebook)

Printed in the USA
CPSIA information can be obtained
at www.ICGtesting.com
CBRC092129220824
13253CB00137B/376